Studland
Old Harry Rocks
Nine Barrow
Matravers
Swanage
Durlston
Tilly Whim Caves

CW00866674

THE WOODLAND CLAN

I would like to thank Arts Council England for supporting the book and trail. Thanks to Ranger Alistair Tuckey of Durlston Country Park and James Gould of Corfe Castle National Trust for supporting the launch of the book and hosting the trail. Thanks to all my creative team* and my sister Margaret whose support and encouragement was constant throughout.
Let us celebrate the voices of

BEAK, BONE, FEATHER AND SONG

..the magical Isle of Purbeck..where spirit and imagination are one..

*Mark Page - Illustration, Sarah Spargo - Book Design, Kevin Benfield - editor, Clare Ambridge - Artist for woodland trail. Chaz Dickie - Musical compositions for the woodland trail.

Chapter 1

THE WOODLAND

A cold and gusty wind swept in over the Isle of Purbeck and swirled into the Woodland. Yellow Hammer, known just as Hammer by all his friends, blew in with it and settled upon the branches of a tree. After a long winter hibernation he had rested his feathers and was now ready for action. *"A little bit of bread and no cheese,"* he chirped. "Where is everyone? Not a thump from Hare or a groan from Badger. Most peculiar," he thought to himself. Thinking he was alone, he began WARBLING and GARBLING, "*A little bit of bread and no cheese.*"

Wagtail and Warbler flew into the Woodland and settled upon the branches. "What a racket!" complained Wagtail. "What a noise!" moaned Warbler. Wagtail asked, "Are you hurt, old chap? Has something ruffled your feathers? Maybe he's hungry?" "A fat juicy worm will settle this nonsense," suggested Warbler. "MARCH MADNESS," they both chirped. Then Linnet and Skylark flew in to join them. "What's ruffled his feathers?" asked Linnet. "MARCH MADNESS," garbled Wagtail and Warbler. "But it's time to fly," said Skylark." "Come on Hammer," they chirped. And all the birds flew around the woodland whistling with excitement. "Stop," said Hammer. "Fellow SKY CLAN, can you see why I'm WARBLING, why my feathers are ruffled?" The birds looked blankly at each other. "The SPRING MOON grows. The flowers are ready to pop but where is EARTH CLAN? Not a thump from Hare nor a groan from Badger. It's most peculiar." "The Swallows have returned," said Linnet. "So have the Sand Martins," added Skylark. "We're missing someone," said Hammer. The birds garbled and thought to themselves. "Blackbird!" they all chirped. "I knew it. I could feel it my feathers," garbled Hammer. "If Blackbird doesn't sing the song of spring then how can spring be sprung?"

Linnet said, "I'll do it. I have a voice just as good as Blackbird's. I've sung in Palaces and Pavilions. Leave it to me, SKY CLAN. I'll wake up EARTH CLAN with my glorious song!" And Linnet flew around the Woodland whistling wildly. "You're too squeaky," complained Hammer. "Why don't you try?" squawked Linnet. "I'm sure *a little bit of bread and no cheese* will wake up the Woodland!" Well, this RUFFLED Hammer's feathers and the two began garbling at each other. "MARCH MADNESS," chirped the birds. Skylark flew in between them. "SKY CLAN, think who can warble like Blackbird?" "Well, not me old chap. I'm a bit cheepy," said Warbler. "And I'm too chirpy," added Wagtail. "We'll never do, us two," the pair garbled away. "Well, there's only one thing for it!" said Hammer. "I will fly to Arne and look for Blackbird. Spring has to be sprung. And while I don't have the voice of Blackbird, I have the brains." And with a whistle, Hammer flew off to Arne. Now, **Small Foots,** while Hammer flies to Arne, I must tell you the story of Blackbird and how he got his orange beak...

Chapter 2

BLACKBIRD VOICE OF SPRING

Many moons ago, Marigold, a farmer's daughter, went missing. It happened one spring day as she was walking home from her friends. Marigold loved flowers; she was named after one. Her flame orange hair and eyes of iris blue made her look like a flower. She loved to run through the meadow, picking the wildflowers which she would take home to her mother. If she was late, her mother would tell her off saying, "No dinner for you. It's burnt to a crisp." But then Marigold would place the flowers on the table saying, "These are for you, mum", and then she could do nothing but hug Marigold.

But on a beautiful spring day Marigold went missing. Her mother waited for her, thinking that perhaps she was in the meadow making daisy chains. But when darkness fell, her mother panicked. What had happened to her daughter? Well, **Small Foots,** Marigold had been dancing in the meadow as she did most days. But on this day the Lord of the Underworld – the Lord of the world beneath us, hidden in the realm of shadows – was riding past on his horse. In the cracked earth he heard her say, "Oh, I wish I were a flower that grew from the ground," and with that, he sucked Marigold into the ground and rode away.

That night the whole village came out looking for Marigold. Had she become trapped in Tilly Whim caves, drowned at high tide or worse, had she been murdered? Torches were lit. People prayed that Marigold would return home safely. But days and months passed by; still no sign of her. Her mother never gave up and every day she went to the meadow to look for her daughter, calling her name as loud as she could. "Marigold, can you hear me? Marigold, are you alive?" Heartbroken, she fell to the ground crying and Marigold, who was underground, could hear her making the earth shake with grief.

”Mum, I’m alive. I’m alive.” But her mother couldn’t hear her. Marigold was alive and living underground in a realm where everything was in shadow. The Lord gave her a room. She had a candle for light, a warm fire, food, anything she wanted. He wanted a bright flower to light up his world and Marigold was that flower. Though he mined diamonds worth millions, she was the jewel of all jewels. Here she would be Queen. “I want to go back home to my mother who’s waiting for me. I miss her. Why have you taken me?” and he replied, “You wished it. What’s done is done. Here you’ll be Queen. What more can you want?” “My freedom to run through the wildflowers,” she replied but all her pleas were ignored. “You will be my Queen. ” And with that he reached up his arm and plucked from the shadows a bird as black as coal and whispered, “Guard her. If she escapes, I will pull off your wings.” The bird blinked in fear and flew towards Marigold following her every move.

Months passed and snow fell upon the earth. Marigold was soon to be married and Blackbird didn’t let her out of his sight. She passed her time making herself a dress, sewing on colourful silk flowers. Watching the spring roots grow underground, she began guessing the flowers, "That's a daffodil. I can smell it from here. I'm going to sew one on here, bright yellow gold. This place is so gloomy, even the birds are black." And she began to cry. Now Blackbird had been captured long ago and he too was a prisoner. He felt sad for Marigold. To comfort her he decided to sing. And what a voice he had, **Small Foots.** Marigold stopped crying and started dancing. She imagined herself dancing in the meadow.

Over time, Blackbird and Marigold become close and, instead of guarding her, he took care of her. They would look up and imagine the meadow with its wildflowers. Spring was coming and so was Marigold's wedding. "It's not that I don't care for him. He has given me everything, diamonds and riches that I could never have had as a farmer's daughter. But I miss my mother." Blackbird pecked away at the earth. It crumbled away. The pair looked at one another and saw their freedom. Every day, as Blackbird sang, Marigold would scrape a hole.

Within three days she had tunnelled a hole so wide that at sunrise you could see the sun stretching its rays down to Marigold's room. Marigold whistled at Blackbird who flew to her. *"Promise me, Blackbird, when we are free, you will sing the song of spring." And she kissed the bird, turning its black beak orange, as orange as Marigold's hair. "Fly towards the light," she said.* Blackbird flew up the tunnel as Marigold started to climb up upon the roots and branches. As she climbed, she heard a voice coming from above, "Marigold, I miss you, oh my beautiful child, are you alive?" "Mum, I'm here." And she scrambled up the tunnel and climbed out into the light of the meadow. She could see her mother calling her name. "Mum," she screamed. Her mother, hearing her voice, turned around but as she turned, Marigold transformed into a flower. Her wish had been granted.

Blackbird meanwhile had flown up and settled on the pine tree. He watched Marigold swaying in the breeze. As the years passed Marigold's mother, who by then was old, would walk up to the meadow to see if she could catch a glimpse of her daughter. But there was no sign of Marigold and her mother would say, "Marigold are you alive?" and a voice whispered on the breeze, "I'm here, mother. I never died." Now, **Small Foots,** let's see if Hammer has arrived at Arne… ☙

Chapter 3

BLACKBIRD'S BABES

Hammer arrived at Arne. He hopped from pine tree to pine tree busily looking for Blackbird. "No sign of him. Not feather nor tail, note nor song. *A little bit of bread and no cheese,*" he WARBLED, *"a little bit of bread and no cheese."* "Hammer," barked Deer. Hammer flew up like a firecracker. *"Your feathers are ruffled,"* said Deer. "I should think they are," garbled Hammer, "giving me the frights." Hammer settled himself on the branch and puffed out his yellow chest. "I'm looking for Blackbird. Have you seen him?" "I've seen neither feather nor tail, note nor song of him," said Deer. "The SPRING MOON grows and we should all be gathered in the Woodland," garbled Hammer. "Look to the pine tops." And Deer carried on munching on a juicy green fern. Hammer flew up and flitted from tree to tree until he found what he was looking for – Blackbird perched upon the branches of the pine tree.

"Where have you been? We've seen neither feather nor tail, note nor song from you." Blackbird was silent. "What's wrong. Have you lost your WARBLE? The SPRING MOON grows and the flowers are ready to pop. It's your job as Sky Clan to wake up the Woodland. They're all still fast asleep, I mean …," Hammer hammered on. "I can't sing," replied Blackbird. "MARCH MADNESS," chirped Hammer. "I can't leave my babes," explained Blackbird. Hammer hopped onto the branch and peered into Blackbird's nest. "Why aren't they warbling, hungry for wrigglers?" Blackbird replied, "They were hungry *little warblers* until I fed them seed or what I thought was seed. Turned out to be glass left by the **BIG FOOTS.** Now they're not moving." "Where is your mate?" asked Hammer. "She flew off. She couldn't bear to look at her chicks. You see why I cannot sing. It has left me mute," Blackbird said. "I'm sad for you fellow Sky Clan," replied Hammer. "But you are not to blame. It's those **BIG FOOTS.** We must do something before the spring moon wanes or spring won't be sprung. I will fly back to Durlston and call Hare to wake up EARTH CLAN. You must bring your babes to the Woodland where we will all gather at sunset." Now, **Small Foots,** whilst Hammer flies to Durlston, I would like to introduce you to Raven… ∽

Chapter 4

RAVEN SEER OF VISIONS

Raven arrived in Corfe on the shoulders of Viking hero, Ivar Blood Axe. Ivar was the bravest of all Vikings and was given the name Blood Axe for killing so many men in battle. Many believed his success in battle came from his Raven. She had been given to him by the Norse God, **ODIN. ODIN** was so impressed by Ivar's bloody victories and all the dead souls he sent him that he commanded Raven to watch over Ivar's soul.

She was there to protect Ivar and she had many gifts to offer. She had the power to see the future. **A SEER,** she could tell when it was a good and favourable time for battle. Part of SKY CLAN, she was akin to the wind which guided her. If the wind flowed free and easy, then it was a favourable time to attack and the gods were with them. If the wind was choppy and changeable, then it was unfavourable. Raven would fly high if favourable. The warriors knew when she was ready to scour the battlefield and gather up the souls of the dead in her black winged cloak. She would carry these souls to Valhalla and give them to ODIN. ODIN would count every single one of them. The more souls his kingdom possessed, the more powerful ODIN became. Odin would send Raven back to Ivar to protect him once more.

Raven journeyed between two worlds, Odin's and the Vikings'. As she returned to earth, Ivar would laugh and cry out, "The gods favour me. My mistress has returned," and he would pick up his axe and show off his warrior's skills. When the Vikings came to Studland on long boats from Norway, the villagers of Studland cried out in fear. Ivar stepped off his boat on Studland shores and picking up a stone held it in his hands saying, "Now this land be Viking land," and this made his warriors cry out,

'IVAR, BLOOD AXE, VIKING WOLF.'

The bonfires were lit and the warriors prepared for battle. They looked at maps and planned to take the kingdom of Corfe away from the Saxons. Raven was called to do her work. "Now, Mistress, take to the sky. Be the gods for or against?" And with that, Raven lifted to the skies and headed to Corfe. She flew over Studland, her black winged cloak shadowing the green fields. She imagined the dead souls she would collect for Ivar. But as she approached Corfe and circled over the castle something happened. She began spiralling, tumbling out of the sky. Her black cloak spinning like a whirlwind. She spiralled and landed in darkness. The place was black, as black as Raven's wings. Lost, she began crowing and looking for a way out. Then she heard a voice. "Have you come to take my soul?" A young girl stood in the dark. "They think I'm a witch but I ain't. Just see things, that's all. Get told things, on the wind. I warn 'em, tell 'em, say the wind told me that a long boat was coming and now they're angry but it ain't me, it's the wind. The wind is how I caught you."

Raven gazed at the girl reflected in her blue eyes she saw the girl floating in a pool of water. "Can you hear 'em, the voices, screaming in the dungeon's walls? They told me you'd come, the voices. They told me that you'd save me, take me with you." Raven's cold heart melted. She began crowing and the girl just laughed. "Hush," she said. And with that, she lifted up Raven who flew up out of the dungeon. Raven flew back to Studland. All she could think about was the young girl. She was A SEER just like her; they were the same. If she called battle maybe she could save the girl. Raven was unsure. It was a changeable choppy unfavourable wind but Raven decided to go against the gods and flew high. Ivar was waiting for Raven, "Where is the bird? Why do the gods delay us?" But in the distance Ivar could see her black cloak pass above them. "My mistress has returned and she is flying high. Get ready for battle, sharpen your swords. Beat the war drum. Tell the Saxons to prepare for ODIN. He's ready for their souls to arrive." And with that he lifted his axe up and cried, "Death to the Saxons." The Viking army marched towards Corfe carrying weaponry that would ensure victory.

The Saxon army were ready, prepared with shields of steel and broad iron swords. Ivar cried out his battle call as Raven swooped in and began circling over the castle, waiting for souls. Ivar fought, wielding his axe. He began tearing the Saxons limb from limb like a savage dog. But in his frenzy what he failed to see was the Saxon chief, high up in the turret, taking aim with his arrow. It shot Ivar straight between the eyes. Raven crowed madly. Her master had fallen and she watched as his soul rose angrily out of his body screaming, 'ODIN.' Raven swooped down and scooped up his soul. As she flew past the river, she could see the girl floating in a pool of water. She swooped down once more and scooped up her soul too and carried them both back to ODIN.

She passed into the cold icy realms of Valhalla where ODIN'S wolves howled as she entered. ODIN welcomed her in, saying, "Raven, what do you bring me?" Raven opened her cloak and the soul of Ivar and the girl leaped out. Ivar was shouting, "I'm fallen" and the girl was shivering with cold. "Ivar." cried ODIN. "You are in VALHALLA. Come, bravest of warriors. Feast at my table." And with that, Ivar picked up his axe and began showing off his battle skills. Raven and the girl followed but ODIN turned to her and said "You, Raven, went against me. You are banished from VALHALLA. Go and take that Saxon child with you." ODIN called his wolves and they began barking and chasing Raven, who lifted her black winged cloak, gathering up the Saxon girl within it. Raven headed back to Corfe. When they arrived Raven and the soul of the girl settled upon an ash tree. "Now we are both lost," she said, "two lost souls." And with that Raven wrapped her wings of black around her... Now, **Small Foots,** let's return to the Woodland... ∽

Chapter 5

Silent Sorrow

Sky Clan and Earth Clan stood silent in the woods at Durlston. They had just woken up from a deep winter's sleep only to hear the sad news of the chicks' death crowed by Raven. Blackbird's babes lay motionless and mute on the grass. "They should be WARBLING AND GARBLING," said Hare. "Hungry for wrigglers," squeaked Mouse. "It ain't right. **BIG FOOTS,** I curse 'em all," said Badger.

Raven hovered over the Woodland. It was her duty as SEER OF SKY CLAN to take the chicks to the land of GREAT SPIRIT, a place far beyond the horizon. Here the *spirit of the wild wood* would once again breathe life into them. Raven swooped into the glade. "Wait," squawked Blackbird. And he pulled from his breast three black feathers and placed a feather on each of them. "Now, fly again in the sky of GREAT SPIRIT." The wind whistled through the Woodland. Raven scooped up the babes in her black winged cloak and began her journey to the world far beyond the horizon. The animals raced to follow her.

At the cliff tops of Old Harry the sun was setting like a golden yolk, dissolving fast into the sea. They watched Raven as she became smaller and smaller until she too had disappeared. A cold wind blew through the rocks. It whipped up a wave that frothed and rolled like a wild dog. Owl flew off the cliff tops and headed back to Durlston. Blackbird flew back to Arne. All the creatures returned to their homes. That night Hare sat under her hazel tree and gazed up at the sky. "It is a dark, sad night," she thought. Then she spotted three stars shining brightly. "The chicks have arrived. I will tie three feathers onto my tree to thank the *spirit of the wild wood* for giving them life anew." And so she did and then she curled up in her burrow and fell fast asleep. Now **Small Foots,** as the Woodland sleeps, I must tell you why Owl is the oldest and wisest creature in the Woodland...

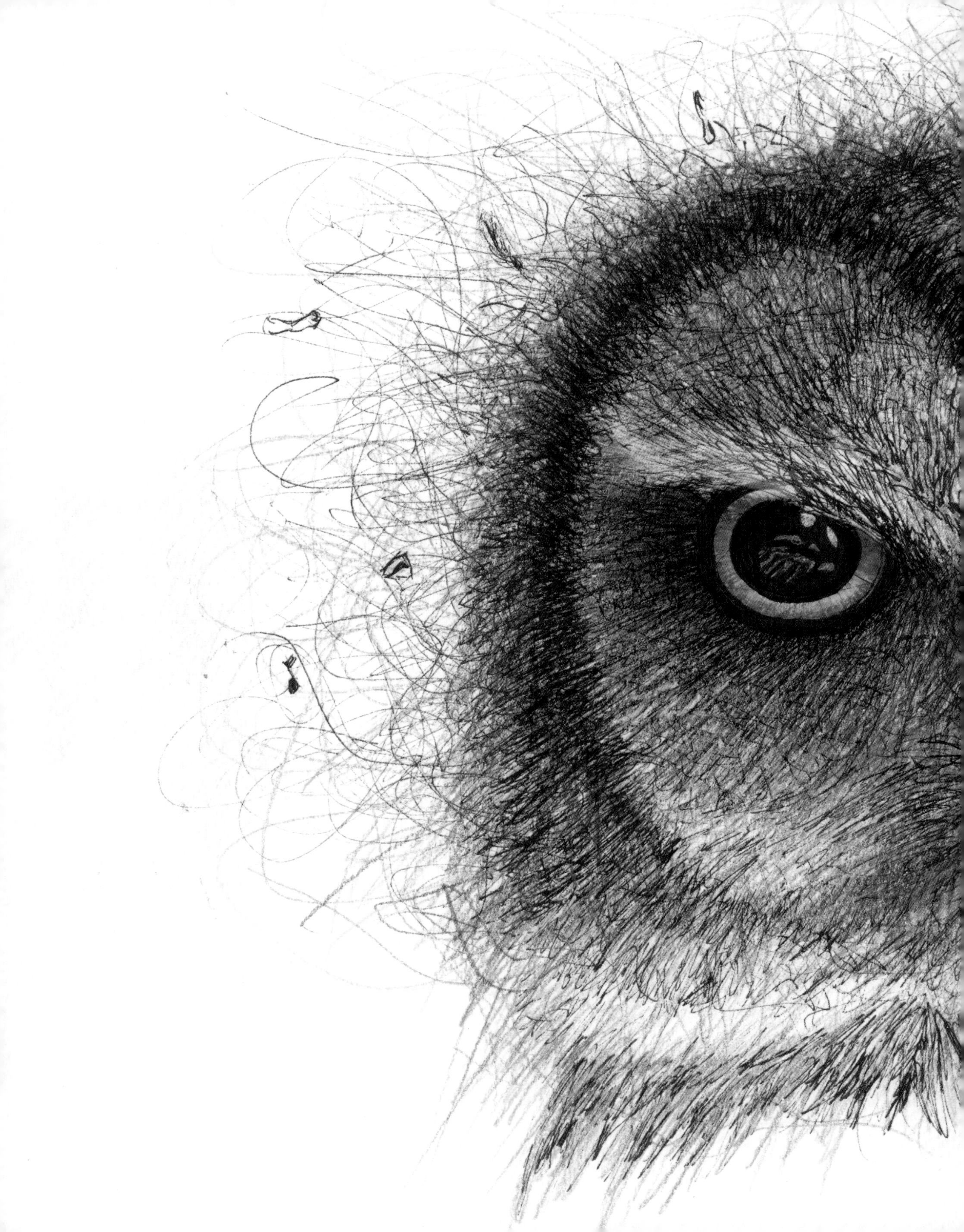

Chapter 6

Owl Guardian of the Woodland

Nobody knew how old Owl was. The creatures of the woods believed him to be as old as the woods themselves and that was extremely old, old as the rocks of Old Harry. Owl has seen a thousand sunrises and a thousand sunsets. He has watched as the tides turn high and low.

You see, **Small Foots,** Owl's eyes recorded everything. So with all that he has seen you can imagine he was rather wise and that is why the creatures looked to him for guidance. But, **Small Foots,** there is another reason why Owl has lived so long. I shall let you into a secret, the secret of Owl's immortality. Many moons ago, when the woods were just tiny green shoots, there lived a man of magic named RAH. He was an alchemist and loved to mix up potions to help and heal the **BIG FOOTS.** He settled in the woods at Durlston and made his home at one with nature. He learnt everything about the woods – its plants and its herbs. RAH'S spell pot bubbled with magic. He was always creating something new – a new cream, medicine or elixir. He would work night and day, mostly at night. He believed the moon shone magic, magic that he needed for his potions. So, when RAH was working alone in the woods, he needed a companion and so he found Owl.

Owl would watch RAH making his potions. RAH saw that Owl was a keen observer. He made him record all the ingredients, methods and spells as well as the phases of the moon. Owl became the keeper of all RAH'S secrets so when he forgot something RAH would ask, "Master Owl, open your eyes and remember for I, a fool, have forgotten." And Owl would open his eyes wide and reflected in them were all the potions he had recorded – the ingredients, methods and spells as though he was making the potion for the first time. This, you can imagine, was really helpful for RAH because he was old and his memory was fading like the waning moon.

He started to have nightmares, dreams of lying on the Woodland floor covered in earth. RAH panicked. He thought he was going to die but he had remembered a potion that every alchemist dreams of making – the *Elixir of Life*, a potion that, once drunk, would allow you to live forever. RAH busied himself day and night, searching for the ingredients to create this elixir. He became obsessed, getting Owl to scour the land for every plant and flower. Each night he would drink the elixir to see if it worked but nothing, no sign of his heart pounding, no urge to race through the wild wood. There was no quickness of breath or growing of bone. If anything, the potions were making him sick. When he looked into Owl's eyes, all he could see was a boney, toothless, old man. "Where is my mind? My mastery? I cannot remember a thing, I've the brain of a flea, the memory of a mouse. All is lost, my friend. I have seen it. I'm crumbling like rock."

RAH knew he was going to die. He sank down. He covered his boney brow with his hands and opened his alchemist's book. A golden leaf flickered on the page, "That's it, Master Owl, don't you see? The final ingredient is gold. Go scour the rocks and find this metal that I may pound to dust. Open your eyes. Look to the rocks for it is there, hidden in stone. Find it before I turn into dust and bone." Owl's eyes blazed like a bonfire as he flew off into the night. A full moon lit up the land. But with a full moon comes a stormy sea.

Owl approached the rocks at Winspit. He hovered over the cliff tops. He could see layer upon layer of grey stone but no gold. The tides pulled upon him but he resisted until he was dragged down towards the rocks into a cave. Owl opened his eyes and lit up the cave. The caves glistened with water. There were rock pools where tiny pieces of flints, shimmered like the sun. It was gold. Owl picked up the gold, clasping it in his claws. Then, when the tide pushed out, he flew up, out of the cave, ascending into the night sky. The moon echoed his cries of delight as he hurried home like a thief carrying a jewel. He arrived back to Durlston and found RAH curled up like a sleeping cat. Owl settled on his master's book and released the gold like jewels from a purse. RAH was awestruck. "My friend help me. Gather my herbs and my pestle to pound. I must mix while the moon is full. I've some breath left yet. Quick, quick as quicksilver." And with that, Rah began pounding the gold and making the potion, repeating over and over the magical words,

"Live, live eternal life – gold is forever as the breath of life."

Owl watched closely. He observed everything. He recorded until the potion was complete. RAH was exhausted. He had used all his breath on the spell. He looked at Owl, smiled, then fell to the ground, the elixir spilling all around him. Owl hovered over his Master. He licked the elixir from the floor and with his beak placed droplets of it into RAH'S mouth but it was too late for Owl could see Rah's heart was silent. He stood by his Master. Then a strange thing happened. Owl felt odd. He felt his heart racing, his feathers growing. A force of life took hold of him so strong he couldn't contain it. So, he flew out of the woods up to the sky. He touched the stars and the moon. He flew from sunrise to sunset. He couldn't stop, a fire was burning within him. Then, one cold winter's night, he finally stopped. He settled himself upon the branches of his old Master's oak tree and a fire glinted like gold in his eyes. Now, **SMALL FOOTS,** let's see what the Woodland Clan are up to… ∽

Chapter 7

THE SUMMONING OF OWL

An angry wind blew through the Woodland. The Clans decided it was time to meet and talk freely –what they called *free beak*. Badger and Mouse made their way from Studland burrowing beneath the damp earth. "**BIG FOOTS,** mischief makers," groaned Badger, "all my years in the woodland I see them messin' and a meddlin'. Laying out traps, traps that killed me old Pa. Now they've gone and killed Blackbird's babes. I'll give 'em a fist alright in their rotten faces. Thems bad, maggoty, old crab apples." Mouse scurried along behind him. Her little feet weren't as strong as Badger's who'd been burrowing for years. "Hop on Midge," he groaned. Mouse hopped onto Badger's hairy back like a flea on a dog.

As dusk fell all the Clans were gathered together in the Woodland. Blackbird spoke, "Woodland Clan, I must speak *free beak.* When my babes died I was left mute. I couldn't WARBLE or whistle or trumpet the joy of spring. It was as if I too had died. Now I must speak, for if I don't, I'll burst with anger." "Blackbird," said Hare, "your babes live again in the land of GREAT SPIRIT. Last night I saw three stars shining in the sky." "But they should be here with me, growing into fat little WARBLERS. Can't you see? No one is safe from the **BIG FOOTS.** So I will speak *free beak* and ask what is to be done?" said Blackbird. "We think with our spirit." said Hare. "If they are to understand us, we must open the **BIG FOOTS'** hearts so we can teach them our ways." "Crab apples," spouted Badger, "thems never gonna change. **BIG FOOTS** killed my old pa and now they've gone and killed Blackbird's babes. So I says thems don't belong here."

The Woodland whistled and pounded in agreement. "The **BIG FOOTS** care for us," said Hare. "I've seen their hearts lifted by Blackbird's song." Blackbird ruffled his feathers in anger. "What about my heart?" squawked Blackbird. "**BIG FOOTS** have broken it." "Rotters," shouted Badger, "rotten, maggoty old crab apples. Clear off! Clear out!" Badger punched his fists as SKY CLAN squawked with anger. Hare thumped her foot. "Let us summon Owl. As Guardian of the Woodland, he will know what to do." Now, **Small Foots,** summoning is how the creatures called one another together. In the creature's world there's no such thing as mobile phones so the animals summon. This is their way of sending out an invitation to come to a meeting. It works like this. First you must close your eyes, next imagine the creature you wish to summon and then begin chanting their name. Chanting someone's name is magical. If you do it long enough, you'll summon up the very person you've been thinking about. So the creatures began the chant,

"Owl, Guardian of the Woodland; Owl, Seer of all things; Owl, burn bright as fire."

As they chanted, they imagined Owl and his amber eyes with his feathers that shone like gold. The trees began to rustle. Owl flew into the Woodland and settled himself upon the branches. He opened his eyes, eyes that recorded everything and then he spoke. "I know why you summon me EARTH and kindred SKY CLAN. I'm as old as the rocks. My eyes remember everything and forget nothing." The creatures were in awe of Owl as he towered before them. "I've watched **BIG FOOTS** from sunrise to sunset, from season to season and what horrors I have seen – a Gull choked by floating rubbish; a Hare snared in rusty wire; **BIG FOOTS** fouling our land and sea. Oh waves, oh wind, oh sea, oh sky! I've seen it all. My eyes are worn out.

A Blood Moon grows and with it anger. Fight back! Speak to the **BIG FOOTS** with our voices of *beak, bone, feather and song.* Beast was here before man. We are the wise ones. If we don't, then misery will follow like a dark moonless night. A new day is dawning. I'll see it all recorded. And I'll ask every one of you, "What have you done?" Owl flew off the branches into the dark night sky. The Woodland was silent. Owl had spoken the truth. And you know, **Small Foots,** when someone speaks the truth, be they beast or **BIG FOOT,** there is silence. There was nothing more to say. Now **Small Foots,** while the Woodland thinks about Owl's wisdom, I must tell you how Hare got her long ears...

Chapter 8

HARE SHAPE SHIFTER

Ever wondered why hares are such good runners? Well, many moons ago, when the Woodland was as young as a tadpole, there lived a woman of magic. Some called her a witch but she was a good woman and her name was Hazel. Hazel was born from a hazel tree which is how she was given her name. She was beautiful with long locks of chestnut hair and eyes as bright as emeralds. Many admired her beauty but, more importantly, many admired her ability to grant wishes even more.

Now, every March, when the woods grew green again, Hazel offered the villagers the chance to bring their wishes to her – be it a wish for love, a baby or good crops. She would take their wishes and tie them onto colourful ribbons which she hung upon her hazel tree. In the moonlight Hazel would dance around her tree chanting her magic spells. This would draw in the *spirit of the wild wood* who, upon hearing the wishes, would grant every single one of them. So powerful was her magic, so kind was her heart and her desire to help others that she became admired by all.

For many years she remained in the woods, happy and loved. Then, one March, a village woman asked Hazel to grant her deeply held wish that her sweetheart would ask her to marry her. And so, being a kind woman, she put the woman's wish in with her colourful ribbons ready to tie to her tree. Now, **Small Foots**, it was a windy March day and it was difficult for Hazel to tie all their wishes upon her hazel tree. In her struggle to get all the wishes upon the branches in time for the full moon she accidentally tied some of her chestnut hair within the ribbon. Well, magic being magic, the wish took on the power of Hazel. Under the waxing moon it grew stronger and stronger until the moon was full. All the wishes had been granted in accordance with the villagers' wishes – all but one, the young woman's. She was mad with jealousy as all her sweetheart could talk about was Hazel – Hazel and her beautiful chestnut hair, Hazel and her bright green eyes. She spread lies in the village warning all the women of the village to be careful not to lose their sweethearts to such an evil woman. It didn't take long before this gossip spread and all the women of the village who once had loved her now began to hate her. She was too free, too beautiful, too powerful and not to be trusted.

One night when it was pitch black with not a star in the sky, a group of these women went to the Woodland to teach her a lesson. They found her busy making her magic and she was pleased to see them. Had their wishes come to pass, she wondered? But no, they had nothing kind to say and, in their anger, they took out their axes and began to chop down the branches of her hazel tree. "Stop, what are you doing?" she cried. The women grabbed hold of Hazel and held her down on the ground. They got out their sharp scissors and began cutting off her beautiful locks of chestnut hair. Hazel struggled like a wild animal. "Stop, I beg you. Why are you doing this?" But the women carried on cutting off her hair and then they lunged the scissors towards her eyes. Hazel panicked and used her magic, *"Spirit of the wild wood, transform me from beauty to beast. Away, my spirit is free."* And with that she transformed into a hare. She leapt from the clutches of the women, running into the Woodland so fast that no one could catch her. She ran and she ran, never to return. So, you see why hares run swift as the wind, why they have long ears and bright eyes and why some even have the power to grant wishes. Now, **Small Foots**, let's see if the Woodland Clan has come up with a plan…

Chapter 9

Beak, Bone, Feather and Song

All the creatures in Woodland were left guessing. What did Owl mean by *beak, bone, feather and song?* It was a mystery. Maybe Owl was too wise, too clever for his own good and this made the creatures cross. Badger made his feelings clear, "Owl and his rotten riddles. When I sees 'em I'll badger them alright with a couple of bruising punches. Make em look like crab apples." Thump, thump, thump, Hare pounded her feet. "Owl's right. We must awaken them to our voices. You forget, I was once a **BIG FOOT**. I didn't see the creatures trying to help me, Blackbird's song lifting me to joy, the comforting hoot of Owl. They need us as much as we need them. Can't you see them tapping on machines? No time to watch me hopping through the wild scrub. If only they could lick the dew and roll in the scrub? *They'd all be a hoppin' an' spoonin' like crazy cats."* And with that, the Woodland began hooting and hollering because many a creature enjoyed a good roll in the scrub. Why? Because the earth's dust is full of magic and if you were to roll in it long enough you'd soon find yourself mad with joy. Hare spoke out, "I speak the truth. We can teach the **BIG FOOTS** our ways and our wisdom. When I was a **BIG FOOT**, I longed to be free like the bird in the sky. But I am Hare. I race through the meadow, slip down the sand dunes and roll in the scrub. Such freedom I never knew as a **BIG FOOT** so I say, let them be more like us!"

A shadow crept over the Woodland. Raven hooked herself upon the branches and opened her crystal ball eyes. "I've come casting. Shadows are within me. Can you hear them screaming?

They're driving me crazy like lost souls trapped within dungeon walls." Reflected on Raven's eyes were visions of the future, mountains of rubbish, plastic bags floating in the sea, fires and floods, nothing but earth's destruction. "There's still time to change it," crowed Raven. "A BLOOD MOON rises. Rise with it." Raven flew off the branches and dissolved into darkness. "No peace now," spouted Badger, "we must burrow deep and let the **BIG FOOTS** die." "BLOOD MOON," answered Hare, "that's what Owl said. A BLOOD MOON is rising and we must rise with it. Our voices can change the future. We have the power, the animals have the power." Hare thumped her foot and began chanting. *"Beak, bone, feather and song – we are the Woodland we are one."* The Woodland joined in and the beat grew stronger and stronger. And soon they were rolling in the dust. Imagine, **Small Foots**, playing your favourite song full blast. Well, this is how the animals felt, they were hoppin' and a rollin', spoonin' like crazy cats to the brightest of beats, a beat that had the power to change the world. Now, as the Woodland parties, I must tell you how Badger got his stripes...

Chapter 10

Badger Hidden Hero of Studland Bay

Badger burrows underneath the green paths of the Coastal Path, serious, determined, focused on his job. To be honest, **Small Foots**, Badger has the best of both worlds. He could go up to the Woodland and take in the smell of the bluebells, then back down to the dark earth which kept him cool in summer and warm during winter. You may walk through the Woodland and wonder where he is when you see an empty burrow with no one at home. Well, he's busy, tunnelling away, mostly at night, while the rest of the world lays fast asleep. Badger is as black as coal. Some believe he was given his stripes by THE MOON GODDESS who, one night watching him run through the woods, cast down a silver beam zigzagging across his back. Badger is the toughest of all the creatures in the Woodland. How can that be? He's half blind, hidden underground in darkness. Well, take a closer look at Badger. See his razor-sharp claws, his thick black snout and his muscles built up like bricks from years of burrowing. You wouldn't want to get into a fight with Badger. He's fearless and could knock you clean out with one swipe of his paws.

And here, **Small Foots,** is where his story begins in the dark underground tunnels of the Coastal Path. Many moons ago, there lived a man named Rightful Robin. He was called this by the people of Wareham as he showed great kindness to all, especially the poor who at that time worked hard ploughing the land much like Badger. Now these country folks worked from morning to night for rich landowners. They didn't complain until one day the landowner put up the rent for their cottages and this meant they had no money for food. Desperate and hungry, they became involved with smugglers who could get them cheap food. This was dangerous as it was illegal to smuggle goods but the people felt they had no choice and so they carried on. Then one night a boat carrying goods was spotted off Old Harry. Smugglers were seen lifting tubs of goods, tea and sugar. A coastguard spotted them and blew his whistle. The smugglers were arrested and the town was on fire with gossip. The poor workers were hauled into court and given ten years in prison as a punishment. Rightful Robin heard the sentence and begged the judge to release them, explaining why they had been forced to buy food from smugglers. It was, as he said, "the greedy, pocket thieving landowners who were to blame." The judge was furious and decreed that Rightful Robin was a troublemaker and a traitor. He sentenced him to death by drowning which meant that within three days Robin would be placed in a sack, wrapped in chains and thrown off the cliff tops at high tide. Rightful Robin was taken to Coastguard's Look Out to await his death.

Night fell and in the Woodland Badger burrowed. It was bitter cold and all the creatures were curled up fast asleep, all apart from Badger. Mouse was sheltering in the Coastguard's Look Out and heard Robin asking God to forgive him. "Lord, forgive me, I meant no wrong, just wanted the poor to be heard. Take my soul quick, before the chains sink me deep below." Mouse scurried up to Robin who whispered, "Tiny thing. Have you come to keep me company? If only you could save me." But Mouse had a plan. She scurried off and went to see Badger. "It's nothing to do with me," said Badger, "**BIG FOOTS** are always killing one another. That is their way." "But he has a good heart," replied Mouse. "He has tried to help the poor, those who are hungry and whose voices are unheard." Badger felt sad for Robin. He remembered his own father snared in a trap set out by the **BIG FOOT'S**, the pain and suffering of a prisoner waiting to die. "We need to free him," said Mouse. "You can burrow

,,a tunnel from Studland Bay to the Coastguard's Look Out. There he can make his escape." "But that will take me a whole moon," said Badger. "Eek," exclaimed Mouse, "you have three days," and with that Mouse scurried off. "Best get started," thought Badger. And he shook of the dusty earth and dug in his claws.

Three days flew by and I can tell you, **Small Foots**, once on a mission Badger is unstoppable. Like a superhero full of muscle and power, he persisted and burrowed a tunnel from Studland Bay all the way to the Coastguard's Look Out. It was the night before the execution and Rightful Robin kneeled, praying, "Lord, make it quick, so I don't feel the cold of the water. Take me before I sink to the depths below." Mouse scurried in and looked at Robin. He observed the tiny mouse, "Think me not a coward. I'm not scared to die, it's just the water I'm afraid of." Then Robin heard scratching. It was deafening. From out of nowhere the floorboards exploded and out popped Badger with muddy snout and squinting eyes. Mouse scurried over to a hole as wide as the moon's crater. Robin peered into the tunnel and saw his escape. "Who would think a Mouse and Badger would be my saviours?" and with that, Robin climbed into the tunnel that would lead him to freedom.

Robin followed Mouse and Badger, crawling and whistling his way down the dark passages of earth. He felt scared but the more he whistled the more he sensed his freedom. He could hear the echoes of sea winds blowing through the passages, the waves crashing upon the rocks. They had reached the end of the tunnel at Studland Bay. Robin crawled out of the tunnel into the cave. He saw a light shine down upon him. Owl's amber eyes lit up the cave. He was free. Robin was never seen again. Some say he set sail on a boat bound for France and he lived there a free man. As for Badger, well he wasn't interested in glory but he did feel super proud of his tunnel, his muscles and getting one over on the **BIG FOOTS**. Now, **Small Foots**, let's see what the Woodland Clan are up to… ☙

Chapter 11

Błood Moon Uprising

The BLOOD MOON ripened like a strawberry. *"Beak, bone, feather and song,"* chanted Hare as she scratched out her plan in the earth. The earth's dust made her fur tingle with excitement. In the Woodland, Hammer was busy organising SKY CLAN. He reminded them, "Hare said we must WARBLE loudly. So fellow SKY CLAN let us all WARBLE together." Hammer puffed out his yellow breast and the birds began warbling. Linnet warbled higher and higher. "What are you doing?" squawked Hammer. "You said WARBLE loudly," chirped Linnet. "Yes, but not to deafen us." "What's that, old chap?" said Warbler. "I said not to … oh never mind. Can we all try warbling together?" The birds garbled in agreement and started warbling. They WARBLED and GARBLED then WARBLED. Hammer was exhausted. He ruffled his feathers and sank down on the branch. "I'm puffed out," he chirped. But Linnet continued to WARBLE higher and higher. The birds looked on in amazement. "She's as bold as the sun," cheeped Wagtail. "As bright as a buttercup," chirped Warbler." "Squeaky show off," Hammer garbled to himself as he ruffled his feathers.

Meanwhile, at Studland, Badger and Mouse lay snoozing in the hedgerows. "BLOOD MOON'S a comin'. Ain't it time to teach those **BIG FOOTS** a lesson," groaned Badger. Mouse bristled her whiskers in agreement. "Come on Midge, best get a wriggle on." Mouse hopped onto Badger's back and the pair headed off to Swanage. Dusk fell upon the Woodland. Sky and EARTH CLAN gathered to hear Hare's plan of action. "Woodland Clan, can you see the BLOOD MOON burning bright. Tomorrow it will be full of magic and with it our voices. Hare revealed her plan etched in the earth. “Badger, you will burrow from Studland to Swanage. Here in the earth lie wire weeds that the **BIG FOOTS** depend on. You will cut those wire weeds with your razor-sharp claws. “Are we all to die?” squeaked Mouse. “How do us know those weeds ain’t traps and I goes down there and end up dead like my old Pa,” spouted Badger. “Trust me,” said Hare. “The BLOOD MOON will give us magic tenfold. Deer, you will run with me and keep a look out. SKY CLAN, you will stay in the Woodland. When the island falls into darkness it will be us, the Woodland Clan, they will look for. Are we ready to teach those **BIG FOOTS** a lesson?” cried Hare. The Woodland whistled and stamped in agreement.

Owl flew into the Woodland, Raven flew in behind him, they both circled the glade. “I saw this day,” cried Owl. “I foretold it’s coming,” crowed Raven. “Let’s us speak our voices with courage and power.” said Blackbird “Hare has spoken.” said Owl. “Let her lead you. She understands the hearts of the **BIG FOOTS**, what they need to learn. When darkness falls, listen for my call. Now rise like the crest of a wave.” Now, **Small Foots**, prepare, whistle and chant for the BLOOD MOON is full and brimming with magic… ઌ

Chapter 12

The Gathering of the Clans

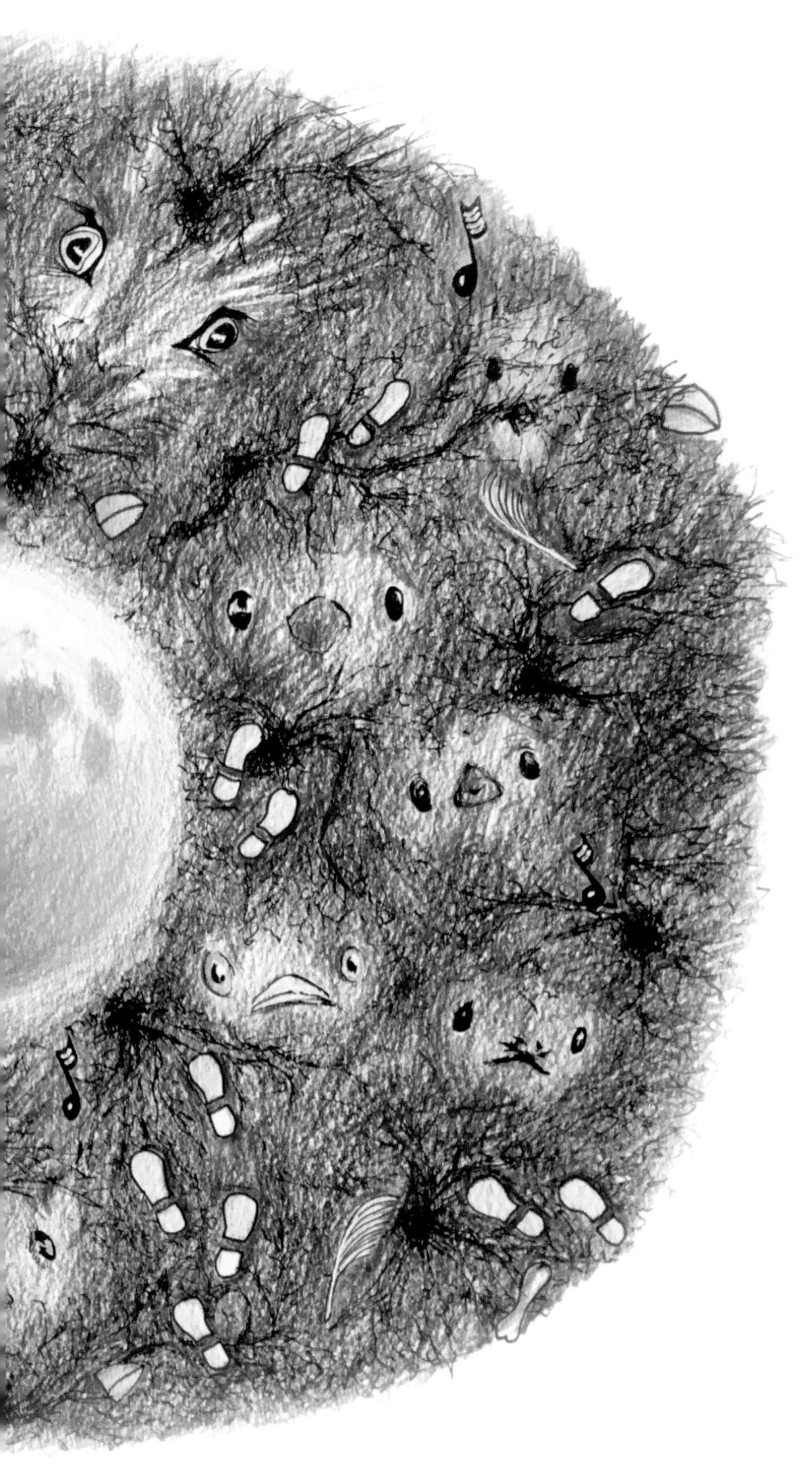

Hare gazed up at the BLOOD MOON. Her heart beat with excitement. She could run from Nine Barrow to Kimmeridge and still be back home in time for sunset. "It's time," she said and began to chant, *"Beak, bone, feather and song."* The sound echoed throughout Purbeck. "Ready Midge?" groaned Badger. As he dug his claws into the earth, it crumbled like a biscuit. Mouse hopped onto Badger's back. The earth's dust fizzed with magic. It made Badger's snout and Mouse's tail explode with power. They felt like a superhero's punching their way through the earth chanting *"beak, bone, feather and song"* and "come on Midge, let's give it some. Smash it." Mouse squeaked with delight as the pair made their way down to Swanage.

Hare was waiting for them. She thumped her foot above the ground and it echoed below. "Hare!" squeaked Mouse. Badger punched a hole in the earth where Hare was waiting. "You see there," pointed Hare, "wire weeds running in the earth? Wire weeds are what the **BIG FOOTS** depend on. Without them they'd be like us." Hare said, "You must cut those weeds and send those **BIG FOOTS** running to the Woodland where they will listen to our voices." Badger wasn't sure, neither was Mouse. "Why don't you cut it?" Mouse squeaked nervously. "Your teeth are sharp and so are your claws." "Right, Midge, I cut em and I'll be frazzle, pop, gone," spouted Badger. Hare laughed, "You're not frightened, are you?" Badger's hairy back rippled with anger. "Right, clear out," said Badger. Hare leaped out the way. "Not you, Midge," Badger groaned. Reluctantly poor Mouse jumped onto Badger's hairy back. "All right, Midge?" Mouse looked down at the wires and with a squeak gave the go ahead. "Right Rotters and no good crab apples, here's a messin'." And with that Badger cut the wires clean in two.

The whole of Purbeck was plunged into darkness. All you could hear were the voices of **Small Foots** and **BIG FOOTS** shouting, "What's happened? Who's switched the lights off? I can't see a thing." Well, you can imagine, **Small Foots**, the mess everyone was in, searching for their phones and not getting a signal. Why? Because SKY CLAN were preventing the Purbeck signals getting through as the birds squawked and whistled over the helpless **BIG FOOTS**. Hare, Badger and Deer ran into the Woodland with Mouse piggybacking on Badger's broad shoulders. Owl flew into the glade with SKY CLAN hooting and hollering the chant. The voices of *beak, bone, feather and song* echoed throughout Purbeck. In the darkness the **BIG FOOTS** heard it like a loudspeaker. They had no phones, no computers, no television to watch, no internet to surf – just total darkness. But in the darkness, they listened as the voices of the animals grew louder and louder. And it made them curious.

The **Small Foots** ran out of their houses to see where the noise was coming from as the

BIG FOOTS shouted, "Come back," but the **Small Foots** had already gone. The chant's magical beat drew them to the woods. **Small Foots** met other **Small Foots** and they started running with excitement following the beat. When they saw the creatures gathered, they were spellbound. In the darkness their bright eyes lit up the Woodland and they watched as the animals beat their chant. The **Small Foots** joined in stamping and clapping *"beak, bone, feather and song – we are the Woodland, we are one."* The beat grew louder. The earth's dusty magic filled the air. The animals and the **Small Foots** were rolling together. When the **BIG FOOTS** arrived they were shocked. But the chant weaved its magic and the **BIG FOOTS** remembered how it felt to be **Small Foots**, to run free in the woods and have no fear. They felt the urge to dance, to clap, to roll in the earth. If only they weren't **BIG FOOTS**! But the beat was too powerful. It made them forget their fears. It made them forget they were **BIG FOOTS** and they chanted *"Beak, bone, feather and song – we are the Woodland we are one."* The whole of the Woodland danced to the beat. Owl opened his eyes as wide as the BLOOD MOON and the animals were silent. Suddenly everything stopped. Mesmerised by Owl's eyes, the **BIG FOOTS** and **Small Foots** gazed up. Reflected on his eyes were all the horrors he had seen. BIG FOOTS dumping rubbish on land and sea, plastic bottles, bags and tin cans, images of animals crying out in pain. Owl's eyes blazed with anger as he showed the **BIG FOOTS** what they had done to the Woodland, what they had done to the world. The more they watched, the more upset and ashamed they felt, each reliving a time when they had stupidly dumped rubbish or accidentally hurt the creatures who hid in fear. The animals' voices grew louder as Owl's eyes recorded the **BIG FOOTS** and **Small Foots** as they each remembered. Then the images stopped. Owl rested his eyes. Hare hopped out of the Woodland into the glade. She leapt towards a **Small Foot** and gazed at her. Unafraid, the **Small Foot** stroked Hare's soft brown ears and all the Woodland was calm. The animals had spoken. Something had changed. ☙

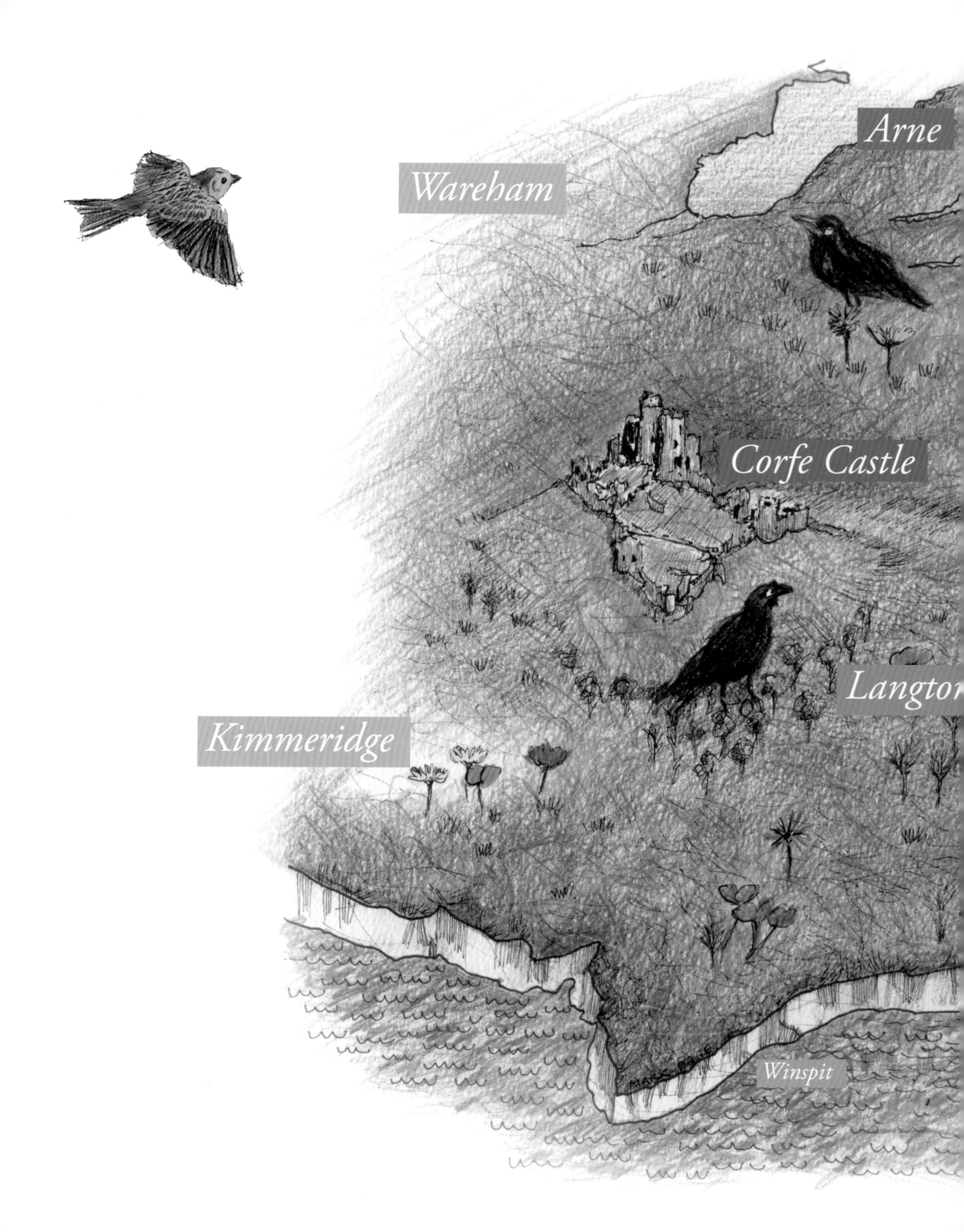
Arne
Wareham
Corfe Castle
Langto
Kimmeridge
Winspit